THE
SECRET
PLAN

Julia Sarcone-Roach

Alfred A. Knopf

New York

made by
Milo

Henry +
Harriet +
Hildy

Milo's adventures with his neighbors Henry, Hildy, and Harriet were always getting interrupted.

There was always something getting in the way.

toppled the tower.

terminated the takeoff.

And sometimes their adventures were
broken up
FOR
NO
GOOD
REASON.

always ruined EVERYTHING.

BEDTIME.

ended the marshmallow roast.

wrecked the great
three-cats-in-a-tree record.

BEDTIME! had to be stopped!

Good thing Milo came up with a
secret plan.

"We'll hide somewhere *before* they call us for
bedtime," he explained.
"If no one can find us, bedtime can't happen!"
"Yep!" said Hildy.
"Perfect!" said Henry.
"Meow!" said Harriet.

So they hid.

And hid.

And hid.

And hid.

And hid.

And hid.

But they kept getting found.

Then they tried going undercover,

blending in,

and wearing disguises of every sort.

They tried sneaking out,

but it was too hard in
the dark,

and, somehow,
they still got caught.

Luckily all that sneaking around gave Hildy an idea. She made sure no one would overhear before she told the others.

"Milo, do you still have those big, furry
monster feet from Halloween?" she asked.
"Of course," he replied.
"Okay then, I've got a new secret plan,"
she said.

That night everyone went about their usual bedtime routines.

They did everything normally. It looked just like they were *really* going to bed.

Milo listened to his bedtime stories and pretended to be super sleepy. He was totally believable.

Then

when

the

coast

was

clear,

When Milo reached the top of
the stairs, he held his breath
and pushed open the
creaky attic door.

Everyone tumbled in.
Hildy discovered a box of hats.
Milo found a suitcase full of mustaches.
Henry began to take pictures.
Harriet studied a book of Morse code.

It was the perfect late-night
no-bedtime-ever hideout.

They celebrated their sneaky escapes with tea fresh off the radiator and a tin of crunchy crackers found in a trunk. But after Hildy's seventeenth cracker and Milo's fortieth cup of tea, everyone began to feel a little sleepy.

"I think I'm ready for bed," Hildy mumbled.

And so, very quietly, they tiptoed back downstairs.

Back in his bed, Milo was just beginning to drift off when he heard a tapping sound.

Harriet was sending him a secret-code message! She had a sneaky, *sleepy* plan.

Milo tapped back his answer,
and a few minutes later . . .

FOR MICHAEL THE MOUSE

Special thanks to Cecile Goyette, Melissa Nelson,
and Nancy Hinkel for their enthusiasm.

THIS IS A BORZOI BOOK PUBLISHED BY ALFRED A. KNOPF

Copyright © 2009 by Julia Sarcone-Roach

All rights reserved. Published in the United States by Alfred A. Knopf,
an imprint of Random House Children's Books, a division of Random House, Inc., New York.

Knopf, Borzoi Books, and the colophon are registered trademarks of Random House, Inc.

Visit us on the Web! www.randomhouse.com/kids

Educators and librarians, for a variety of teaching tools, visit us at www.randomhouse.com/teachers

Library of Congress Cataloging-in-Publication Data
Sarcone-Roach, Julia.
The secret plan / Julia Sarcone-Roach — 1st ed.
   p.   cm.
Summary: Continually thwarted in their efforts to escape bedtime and continue playing, a young
elephant and three kittens finally find a "perfect late-night no-bedtime-ever hideout."
ISBN 978-0-375-85858-1 (trade) — ISBN 978-0-375-95858-8 (lib. bdg.)
[1. Play—Fiction. 2. Bedtime—Fiction. 3. Elephants—Fiction. 4. Cats—Fiction.] I. Title.
PZ7.S242Sec 2009   [E]—dc22   2008039291

The illustrations in this book were created using acrylic paint.

MANUFACTURED IN CHINA
October 2009
10 9 8 7 6 5 4 3 2 1
First Edition

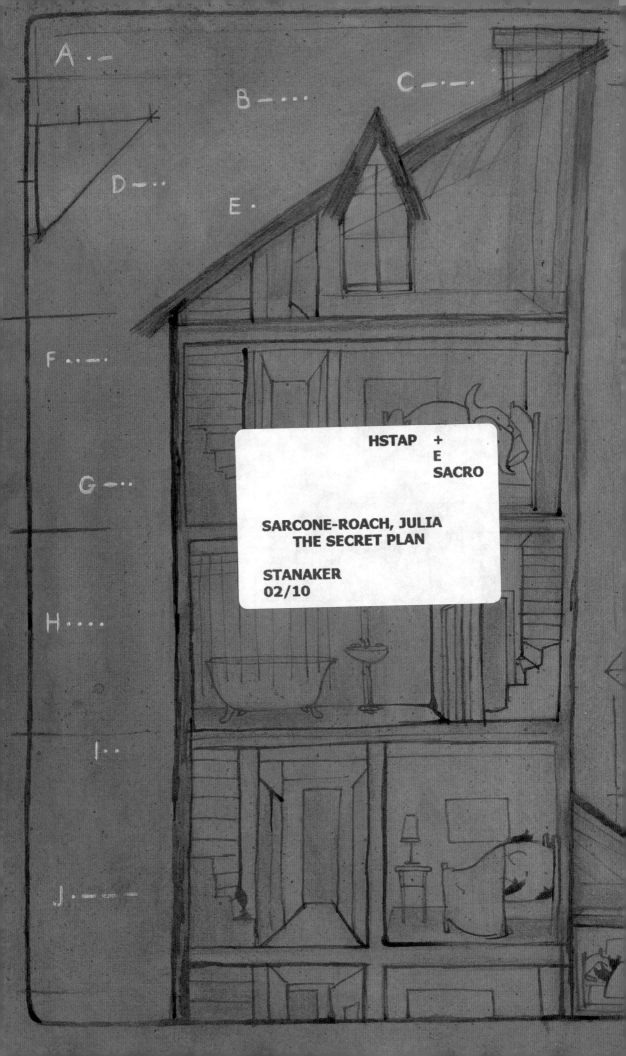